Nightmare Realities

Amanda J Evans
Illustrations by Emma Donnelly.

Handersen Publishing LLC
Lincoln, Nebraska

Nightmare Realities

Handersen Publishing, LLC
Lincoln, Nebraska

Text copyright © 2017 Amanda J Evans
Illustration copyright © 2017 Emma Donnelly
Cover copyright © 2017 Handersen Publishing, LLC
Cover and Interior Design by Nichole Hansen

Manufactured in the United States of America.

This is a work of fiction. Names, characters, places, and incidents are either the products of the author's imagination or are used fictitiously. Any resemblance to actual persons, living or dead, businesses, companies, events, or locales is entirely coincidental.

First Edition

Summary: A collection of scary stories perfect for sharing on dark nights. Are you brave enough to read more than one?

Library of Congress Control Number: 2017953334
Handersen Publishing, LLC, Lincoln, Nebraska

ISBN-13: 9781941429921

Author Website: www.amandajevans.com
Publisher Website: www.handersenpublishing.com
Publisher Email: editors@handersenpublishing.com

DEDICATION

To dream believers everywhere. To making the impossible possible and living the life you desire. To my wonderful husband for all your support and encouragement. And for my talented daughter, Emma, for turning my words into pictures. To my son, Conor, for his patience as these stories formed. To all who helped make this book a reality.

CONTENTS

ACKNOWLEDGMENTS

I would like to thank Nicki and Tevin from Handersen Publishing for all their support and for taking a chance on an unknown writer.

The NGD
The Nightmare Giving Demon

Everyone knows about the BFG. In fact, you've probably seen the movie a dozen times. But what about the NGD? Have you heard of him?

Shall I tell you a little secret?

You see, the BFG isn't real. He's a made-up character to help children feel good about giants. The NGD, however, is one hundred percent real. And he's something you *should* be afraid of.

NGD stands for "Nightmare Giving Demon."

Everyone has one. The day you were born, so was your very own personal NGD.

He follows you around. He sleeps under your bed. And he has one mission: to find your fears and use them against you.

He's listening when you talk to your friends, especially about all those things that make you cringe. He's with you when you jump or receive a fright. He's there beside you, watching over your shoulder, whispering in your ear while you read that scary book at night.

He's the dark shadow you see when you walk alone at night. He's always there, gathering information and waiting for the right time to use it against you.

The cold breeze on your face when there is no wind? You know that feeling, right?

That's him.

The shiver that runs up your spine? Makes the hair on the back of your neck rise? That's him, all right.

When you lie in bed at night with your heart racing, and a sense that something bad is going to happen.

That's your NGD.

He's probably lying under your bed, hoping that you'll put your foot out so he can reach out and grab it.

The eerie sense when someone is watching you? It's your NGD, invisible to the naked eye, even when he's standing right in front of you.

He's always with you. Watching. Listening.

He was there when you watched those horror movies your mom told you not to. He was there when you felt a chill walking past that old abandoned house.

He was the dark shadow you saw in the window when your friends all laughed.

He's gathering up everything.

All your fears are being documented. How you hate clowns, or spiders, or when you hear strange noises coming from the basement.

Your NGD has note of it all. What makes you squirm…what causes your body to tremble in fear…

And when you least expect it, when you feel safe and secure, he will strike. Your heart will race for no reason at all. And *things* will move in the darkness.

When that happens, you'll know he's near. And he's getting ready to pounce. He'll feed on your fear.

When tears form in your eyes.

When you try to move, but can't.

When you call for help…

He'll stop you.

You'll freeze, helpless to do anything but watch as this invisible demon conjures up terrors you'll never escape from.

He is your NGD. The one who watches, who waits for his chance to scare you to death.

Beware the things you say, for the NGD listens to all.

Think good thoughts. Do as you're told. And never, ever let him know what you're afraid of. Because once you do, the Nightmare Giving Demon will have all the power. And you will never sleep with the light off again.

THE END

All Hallows Eve

It was All Hallows Eve, the one night of the year when the dead can roam the earth. The one night when spirits are free to torment the living. When nightmares can become a reality.

"It's the only night we can do this," Fergal said, walking around me in circles. "One night, but anything can happen."

I didn't like the look on his face when he said this, but I couldn't show my fear. I was the new kid, and if I wanted to be one of them, I had to complete their challenge.

"One hour, Johnny, that's all. Your challenge is to sit in the graveyard for one hour," Peter said.

"What's an hour?" I thought. Ghosts aren't real. There's no such thing as this reaper they keep going on about. They're only trying to scare me with their stories of the ghostly figure that haunts the graveyard.

"You know," Max said. "They say that whoever spends more than thirty minutes in the graveyard on All Hallows Eve becomes the reaper's prey, and they're never seen again."

I swallowed hard. "I'll do it. I ain't no chicken."

The boys laughed. "We'll see," they said as I pushed open the creaky gate to the graveyard.

I'd come fully prepared. I'd added new batteries to my flashlight and my phone was fully charged.

"I'll be fine," I told them. "What's the worst that could happen? It's not like there's anything out there. Right, guys?"

Nobody answered. And the fact that they actually looked nervous didn't help.

There was no moon to light my way as I headed into the silent graveyard. The boys moaned and groaned at the gate. I looked back at them, scowling.

"What?" Fergal said, trying to look innocent. "We're just trying to make it more, you know, authentic."

He nudged the others and they all started giggling.

"I'll show them," I thought as I turned into the darkness.

"We'll be back in an hour," Max shouted to me. "Hopefully you'll make it."

What's an hour? It's only sixty minutes. All I have to do is sit down beside that tombstone and play games.

I made my feet move in the direction of the headstone, telling myself to calm down. I hated the dark. It's the one thing that freaked me out, and had been for as long as I could remember. But I needed this to work out. I needed to make friends. It was bad enough having to move here in the first place. The last thing I wanted was to be a loner.

Once I reached the tombstone, I sat down and rested my back against it. It's only sixty minutes, I reminded myself.

The silence was eerie. Nothing moved as I sat in

complete darkness. I checked the time on my phone.

Only fifty-five minutes to go.

I wasn't worried though, because my flashlight could cut through the darkness.

I pulled up Pokémon Go, but quickly decided against it. I wasn't going wandering around here in the dark. I decided I needed something to keep my mind occupied, so I settled on Minecraft. At least that would keep me busy. My hour alone in the graveyard would pass in no time.

The game wouldn't load.

"Come on, stupid phone," I said, exiting and trying again.

From out of nowhere, I heard noises. Soft moaning coming from my right.

"I can hear you guys," I said, knowing it was just the boys trying to scare me.

Checking my phone, I saw that I still had fifty minutes to go.

A sharp scream pierced the air. It sounded like a woman. My body jumped to attention, and I could feel my heart pounding. I hated the dark. I pointed my flashlight in every direction, but there was nothing there. No movement, nothing.

I checked my phone again.

I still had forty-five minutes left.

The tension was getting to me. But I reminded myself that it was all in my head. My mind was imagining things, making stuff up.

I needed a distraction, another game to take my mind off everything. It didn't matter what app I clicked on, none of them would open.

"Come on," I said, tapping the screen harder.

The one time I really needed my phone, it decided to act up. It wasn't long before a fog began to descend on the graveyard. I could barely see through it.

My mind conjured up images of zombies crawling out of their graves, stomping across the earth, intent on eating my flesh.

"Get a grip," I thought.

Then I heard leaves rustling. I sat up straight, eyes wide, trying to peer through the fog. I aimed my flashlight, but there was nothing there. Everything was exactly the same as when I checked a couple of minutes ago. I still had another forty minutes left before I could leave this dreadful place.

"This was such a stupid idea," I said, which got me to thinking. Did I really want these guys as my friends? Heck, I didn't even like them that much.

Alone, in the dark, I questioned everything.

My breathing was erratic, my palms were sweaty, and the fog was getting thicker.

There was a loud moan, followed by a tremendous bang. My body jerked from the noise and my shoulder hit the tombstone behind me.

"Ow," I muttered, rubbing it while looking around. I couldn't see anything. The fog was everywhere, like a smokescreen.

I pointed my flashlight, cutting through the air, but there was nothing there. Nothing moved, nothing stirred. Only silence—except for the noise of my heart pounding in my ears. The fog was getting worse. But the good news was that I only had thirty minutes left now.

"I've got this," I said, trying to psyche myself up. "I'm halfway there."

There was a loud bang, followed by more screams and moans. I kept reminding myself that it was just the boys hiding behind the wall, trying to scare me.

It had to be them.

I pointed my flashlight again, only this time nothing happened. There was no light. I slapped the side of it with my hand, shaking it, but it wouldn't work. I grabbed my phone, so I could use the flashlight on it instead. I slid my finger across the screen, then let out a deep sigh of relief as it came to life. This will do just fine. I swiped up, to find the light.

"Now what?" I said.

My phone's battery warning flashed before it turned off. I pressed the power button again and again, but it was useless. This couldn't be happening. I charged my phone. The battery was full.

Leaves rustled. The sound made me jump, and I held my breath. I was in complete darkness now.

"It's just the boys," I said. "It's just the boys."

Only twenty minutes to go now. I knew I could get through this, if only I could force myself to calm down. My eyes peered into the darkness, looking for anything at all. That's when I saw them…

Shadows.

Moving towards me.

The sound of rustling leaves grew louder, and I knew I'd have to move. My body, however, didn't seem to agree with me. My legs turned to jelly, shaking as I tried to move.

"It's just the boys," I reminded myself. "It's just them fooling around."

I repeated my mantra over and over again as I forced myself to move. I crept towards the gate, crouched down to remain hidden. If the boys were hiding behind the walls, I didn't want them to see me. I'd never live it down if they saw how scared I was.

I had no phone, no flashlight, and the fog was impossible to see through. I knew I'd walked in a straight line from the gate when I came in, so I pointed my feet in that direction.

The moans and screams continued, getting louder and closer. I saw a dark shadow moving in my direction. That's when I decided to run in the direction I *hoped* the gates were in. I'd had enough. I didn't care whether the guys saw me or not. This was just too creepy.

Shadows moving? Women screaming? Fog coming out of nowhere?

"So what if I failed their challenge?" I thought. It wasn't important anymore. All I wanted to do was get out of the graveyard.

My legs pounded the muddy ground as I ran, my eyes wide as I tried desperately to peer through the darkness. My foot sank into the soft earth. When I went to move it, a hand grabbed my ankle.

I couldn't help the scream that left me as I fell to the ground, high-pitched and petrified.

Panic rose inside me.

Every last hair on my body stood to attention, and a cold chill ran down my spine. The temperature must've dropped at least twenty degrees because now my breath was visible.

Desperately, I tried to free my leg from whatever held onto me. I kicked and pulled, but whatever had me…

It wouldn't let go.

The dark shadow I'd spotted was even closer now. I kicked my leg out as hard as I could, finally able to release the hold on my ankle.

It's one of the boys

It's one of the boys

"I know that's you, Fergal," I shouted, trying to stop my voice from trembling. "And you're not scaring me!"

That's when I saw it.

A scythe, cutting through the air. A piece of tombstone landed beside me as the scythe flew through the air again. I scrambled out of the way as a loud scream filled my ears.

The awful scream was followed by a chilling laugh, and I shuddered.

"What was that?" I said.

"You're next, Johnny," a voice whispered. "You are next."

I jumped back. My shoes dug into the dirt as I scrambled to get to my feet. My chest heaved as I watched the scythe move effortlessly through the air, hurtling towards me.

"This can't be happening," I thought. "This can't be happening…" Tears welled up in my eyes and I pleaded for someone—anyone—to help me.

The scythe was getting closer and closer. I curled up into a ball. My hands covered my head as I tried to block out the sound of the screams. The sinister laughter was all around me, mocking me. And the smell of rot filled my nose, making my stomach turn.

"Oh, God, I'm going to be sick."

I lurched forward just as the scythe hit the ground. It rose again as I scrambled on my hands and knees.

Swooping down, it caught the edge of my leg. A sharp pain shot through me. It pulled at me, tearing at my skin as I continued crawling through the muck, desperate to get away.

The gates were in sight. I could see them as I willed myself to keep going.

"You can't run, Johnny," the evil voice said. "You are mine now."

Then a hand reached out to grab me. I rolled to the left, narrowly avoiding its grasp. I was almost there.

Almost at the gates.

My freedom, so close.

The shadow was moving closer, swinging its scythe in the air. His eyes glowed red, and he continued to laugh.

I kept crawling, moving backwards towards the gate. My eyes were fixed on the thing coming towards me. My terror had blocked out the throbbing pain in my leg where the scythe had left a nasty cut. I glanced behind me.

The gates were within reach.

I turned and stretched out my hand, touching the cold hard metal. Then I pulled my body, hard as I could, escape the only thing on my mind.

"You can't leave, Johnny," the voice said. "Thirty minutes and you're mine. That's the rule on All Hallows Eve."

I wrapped my fingers around the cold metal of the gate and pulled with all my might. It creaked open, and I could finally see the glow of the streetlights. I was almost out.

I gripped the gates with every last ounce of strength I had left and started pulling myself through to safety.

"You can't leave, Johnny," the voice whispered in my ear. "Your body will feed the horde tonight."

A cold hand clamped down onto my shoulder.

I watched as his scythe began to fall through the air, ready to cut me in half.

I fell backwards, my eyes fixed on the scythe as it made its way closer and closer, until it finally pierced my skin. Pain ripped through my body. I screamed as his red eyes found mine…and he laughed.

"You belong to me now, Johnny."

Blood gurgled in my throat, no sound escaping, as my life faded away. Darkness took hold and my eyes closed.

"Are you ready, Johnny? You have sixty minutes to prove you're not a chicken. We'll meet you outside these gates when it's all over."

A hand slapped my shoulder. I wrenched my eyes open and saw that I was standing outside the graveyard.

My phone was fully charged, and my flashlight was shining brightly. My hand flew to my chest, looking for blood, a gaping hole.

Nothing there.

I pulled up the leg of my trousers, looking for the gash the scythe had made. Again, there was nothing.

I shook my head, trying to clear my thoughts. Everyone was staring at me. They were waiting for me to begin the challenge. The one I had just barely survived.

"What did you say?" I asked.

Fergal looked at me. "You have sixty minutes to prove you're not a chicken," he said. "Then we'll meet you at the gate when the time's up. God, Johnny, what's with you? It's like you spaced out or something."

Had I imaged it all?

I couldn't have. It was all too real. I'd seen him. I'd felt the scythe rip my leg open. I'd felt it pierce my heart. I could still taste blood in my mouth. I wet my lips as I looked at the boys, who were all waiting for my answer.

Was it a warning? Some kind of premonition? A vision of what was to come next?

It was All Hallows Eve, after all. The night of the walking dead. Now all I had to do was decide if I was brave enough to spend an hour in the reaper's graveyard.

THE END

Grandpa and the Hunt

"Why do we have to go to Grandpa's?" Caitlin asked as her mom placed the last few bags into the car.

"Oh, Caitlin, not now," Mom said as she shut the car door. "You know Grandpa doesn't like to be alone, especially on Halloween. And with Grandma in the hospital, I promised we'd go."

"I promised Laura we'd go trick-or-treating together," Caitlin said, crossing her arms in protest in the back seat.

"You'll have plenty more Halloweens," Mom said. "Grandpa's not getting any younger. And besides, I'm sure he'll have some spooky tales to tell."

Mom started the engine and pulled out of the driveway.

Caitlin didn't care about Grandpa's stories. She huffed and made frustrated noises in the back just to annoy her mom.

She pulled out her phone and quickly sent a text to Laura.

Can't make tonight. Mom's making me go to my grandpa's. ☹

WHAT OMG...Ricky Davis is coming to the party...you are so gonna miss out...text me l8r ☹

Ricky Davis was the one boy Caitlin had a crush on. And now she wouldn't get the chance to hang out with him. Caitlin sent out one last text.

Hate my mom ☹

The drive to Grandpa's house didn't take long. On a normal day, Caitlin would have enjoyed the scenery. The autumn leaves were a combination of reds, yellows, and oranges. Grandpa said he liked the country feel, that it reminded him of his home.

"The house isn't decorated," Caitlin said as she got out of the back seat and slammed the car door.

"Don't start, Caitlin," her mom said, then reached into the back to retrieve the groceries.

"Fine," Caitlin said. She climbed the steps to the front door. "Why doesn't Grandpa like Halloween?"

"Well, maybe if you're nice and drop the attitude, he might just tell you," Mom said as she opened the door. "Dad, we're here!" she called, stepping into the hall.

Caitlin followed. She didn't want to be here, but Grandpa's house was always inviting. She'd loved visiting as a kid. There was always somewhere to explore, and Grandpa had the best library ever. She'd spend hours reading old Irish folktales and legends.

Grandpa was originally from Ireland, but he moved to America many years ago, before her mom was even born.

"In here, love." Grandpa's voice floated out from the living room. "Did you bring chocolate?"

"I did," Caitlin's mom called, then handed Caitlin the bar to bring to him.

Caitlin trudged into the living room. She was still sulking over missing out on her evening, but she couldn't help but smile when she saw her grandpa. He was sitting in his chair in front of a roaring fire.

"Caitlin, me girl, what ya got for me?" Grandpa said, giving her a huge grin.

"Hey, Grandpa," Caitlin said, holding out the chocolate.

"Is that all?" he said, and winked.

Caitlin knew the drill. She moved in to give him a big hug.

"That's my girl," he said, squeezing her tight.

Grandpa smelled of old person and tobacco, but it always brought her comfort.

"I hope you're not missing out on anything important tonight," Grandpa said.

"Nah, nothing special," Caitlin said, shrugging her shoulders. She knew her grandpa would feel bad if she mentioned the party. And besides, it wasn't his fault Grandma was ill.

"Here you go, Dad," her mom said, coming into the room. "Cup of tea."

"Ah, Mary, how did ya know?" Grandpa gave her a wink. "Did ya put a drop of whiskey in it?"

"A small drop, Dad," Mom said, placing the cup in his hand.

"Sit yourself down by the fire, Caitlin." Grandpa motioned to the chair opposite him. "Tell me a story."

It's the same thing he says every time. It's not a story he wants, but an update on her life. Caitlin dropped down heavily onto the chair. It was hard to stay mad when she was here. Her grandpa always made her feel special. And as she told him about school and her friends, she soon forgot about missing the party.

"How come the house isn't decorated for Halloween, Grandpa?"

"I don't believe in all that nonsense," he told her. "Halloween is a sacred night, not a celebration of candy."

"Did you go trick-or-treating as a kid?" Caitlin asked.

"Aye, I did," Grandpa said, then took a big gulp of his tea. "Ah, that's grand."

"So, what was Halloween like when you were a kid?" Caitlin asked.

"Nothing like this, that's for sure," Grandpa told her. "When we were young, we got fruit and nuts in our bags. And there were no fancy costumes, either. An old sheet, or black sack is what we had. We listened to the warnings too."

Caitlin's interest peaked. "What warnings?"

"Ah, ya know. The night of the dead and all that. We steered clear of the graveyard. And we made sure not to speak ill of the dead. Sure, we didn't want them coming after us, now did we?"

Caitlin laughed. But Grandpa's face was deadly serious. "Is that why you don't celebrate Halloween, Grandpa?"

"Oh, no lass. That's a different story altogether," Grandpa said. "I'm in hiding, you see. I can't be drawing attention to myself."

Caitlin raised her eyebrows. What in the world could her grandpa be hiding from?

"Would ya like me to tell ya the story, Caitlin?" Grandpa asked. "It's not for the faint-hearted, mind you."

"Sure, Grandpa," Caitlin said. "Why not?" She may as well listen, since there was nothing else to do.

Grandpa rose from his chair and added more logs to the fire. "It's a long one," he said, then winked at her before calling Caitlin's mom.

"Yes, Dad?" her mom said, poking her head around the door.

"Any chance of a wee drop?" Grandpa asked, holding out the empty tea cup. "Just the whiskey this time, love. I'm going to tell Caitlin, here, some real stories."

"Okay, Dad," Mary said, smiling. "Nothing too bad, though. I don't want her up all night."

"Scout's honor," Grandpa said, saluting her.

Caitlin's mom came back into the room a few minutes later with a small glass of whiskey. Grandpa settled back into his chair, with his glass in one hand and a tobacco pipe in the other.

Puffing away, he cleared his throat. "So, Caitlin. What do you know about the wee folk?"

Caitlin's eyes darted to his. "Little folk? You mean leprechauns?"

"Aye, that be them," he said, balancing his pipe in his mouth.

Caitlin shook her head and grinned. "Come on, Grandpa. You can't be serious. You want to tell me about little green men who grant wishes and give you a pot of gold?"

Grandpa took a deep breath. "No, Caitlin, not that made-up nonsense. I'm going to tell you about real leprechauns. Nasty little buggers, they are. And it's not a pot-o-gold you'd be after when you bump into them, believe me."

Caitlin decided it was better to just go along with him. He was old, after all, and by the sounds of it, a little delirious. She plumped the cushions behind her and settled back.

"Okay, Grandpa," Caitlin said. "Tell me about real leprechauns."

"Good girl. Now, where to begin?" He lifted the glass to his lips. "Ah yes," he said, as if he'd just remembered. "I'd just turned sixteen, and I was courting Sheila Ni Bhrian. I was just coming over the top of Sliabh Na Chullaigh when it happened."

"Hang on," Caitlin interrupted. "Grandma's name isn't Sheila."

"You're right there, lassie. This was before I met your grandma. Before I was banished from my beloved Ireland."

Grandpa's face looked sad, so Caitlin decided not to question it any further.

"Okay, so what happened?" Caitlin asked.

"Well now," Grandpa said, scratching his chin and chugging on his pipe. "I'd just left Sheila's home. She lived on the other side of Sliabh Na Chullaigh, ya see. I was walking back to my house, and I hadn't realised the time. It was only when I got to the top of the hill that I noticed the full moon poking out from behind the clouds. I knew the dangers of being on the hill at full moon, but I was a young lad, barely a man. And that night, I'd made me mind up to ask Sheila to marry me. Sure, I was floating home after kissing her at the gate."

Caitlin listened intently. Her grandpa's voice, soft and lilting, his Irish accent creeping in as he recounted his tale.

"There I was at the top of the hill," Grandpa said, then he cringed. "That's when I spotted the full moon.

But there was nothing I could do except keep walking. That's when I heard it."

"Heard what?" Caitlin asked, leaning forward in her chair.

"The hunt horn, clear as ya like. It's loud, ya know?" Grandpa said, clearly upset as his body shivered. "I tell ya, lass, I was so scared by that point, I was frozen to the spot."

Caitlin waited while Grandpa took another drink.

"Once I heard it the second time, I knew I had to move," he went on. "Mind you, being on top of the hill didn't help, so I jumped in behind the bramble bushes that were on me right. There, I prayed they wouldn't see me. Sure enough, when the horn blew a third time, they all came galloping towards me. Loud as thunder, it was."

"Wait a second, Grandpa," Caitlin interrupted. "I'm confused. A horn sounded? Who came galloping towards you? Where did they come from?"

"Sorry, lass. I keep forgetting you don't know the stories," Grandpa said. "I'm talking about the wild hunt. Ya see, the wee folk live in another dimension called Faery. And every full moon, they have the hunt. They come through our dimension, then go back through a different portal into their own. You'll understand as I tell the story, so listen up."

Caitlin agreed to keep quiet while Grandpa told his story.

"I watched from behind the bushes as hundreds of wee folk on their hounds raced down the hill and then disappeared into thin air. Bewildering, it was. There one minute, gone the next. I should've just gone home, but I was young and foolish."

Grandpa shook his head and reached for his glass. His face looked concerned, even scared, as he looked up at Caitlin.

"What happened next is something I'll never forget, and it's the reason I had to leave my beloved Ireland."

Grandpa swallowed the lump in his throat and leaned forward. "In my stupidity, I followed them. I raced down that hill, faster than lightning. And just like that…" He snapped his finger. "I found myself in Faery."

"Really, Grandpa? What was it like?" Caitlin asked, excited at the idea. "It must have been amazing, all colourful lights and beautiful fairies with wings."

Grandpa wasn't smiling. He looked absolutely serious, as if he truly believed it.

"No, lass. It was nothing like that," Grandpa said. "I found myself in a dark forest. Terrified, I was. It was cold and damp, and sure it was enough to put the heart crossways in me. I tried turning around and running back the way I came, but it was no use. Once you enter Faery, you can't leave from the same spot."

"What happened next, Grandpa?" Caitlin asked.

"It wasn't long before I was spotted," Grandpa continued. "A human in Faery is forbidden, and I found that out the hard way. I'd been standing there less than two minutes when I felt something wrap around my legs. I tried to get out of it, but the tree had me. I was strung up, arms and legs spread out, dangling in the air. That's when I met his majesty, King Brian."

Caitlin had heard of King Brian, ruler of all the leprechauns. But she thought it was only a myth.

"Then what happened, Grandpa?" Caitlin asked. "Did they let you go?"

"Aye, they did, but not in the way you're thinking," Grandpa told her. "It was the night of the hunt, remember? They have their rules and I broke them. I broke their sacred laws, making me the hunted. Branded me and all, they did."

"Branded?" Caitlin asked.

"Aye," Grandpa said, lifting his shirt to reveal a large burn-type scar across his stomach.

Caitlin raised her hand to her mouth. The scar was awful. It looked extremely painful.

"It's all right, lass. I don't feel it anymore," Grandpa told her. "Only on hunt nights. That's when it burns."

"But how did you escape, Grandpa?" Caitlin was horrified by the shrivelled skin that covered his stomach. Her mind raced as she tried to think of what might have caused it.

"I was strung up, hovering above the ground," Grandpa went on, "with King Brian standing below me with his hound. Fierce creatures, they are. Ugly, too. The darn thing growled and snapped at me. All King Brian did was laugh."

Grandpa closed his eyes and the images from that fateful night filled his mind. In an instant, he was transported back to Faery, once more dangling from a tree.

"So, young man, what's your name?" King Brian asked.

"Michael O'Riordan," I said as I tried to free myself from the branches.

"Well, Michael O'Riordan," he said, rubbing his hands together. "Welcome to the hunt. The rules are as follows. You have until sunrise to find your way out of Faery. Do that and you are free."

"That'll be easy," I said, trying to appear brave.

King Brian started laughing.

"What's so funny?" I asked.

"Well, Michael, the funny thing is, no one ever makes it out of Faery. Not when they're part of the hunt. The hounds are hungrier than usual too. They haven't had human flesh for many a decade," he said, patting the beast on the head.

The hound snapped at the air beneath my feet, so I lifted them as high as I could.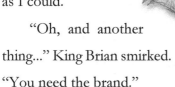

"Oh, and another thing..." King Brian smirked. "You need the brand."

"The what?" I didn't like the sound of that one bit.

"This…" King Brian laughed, raising his hands in the air. He said something I couldn't understand.

In seconds, my skin started to heat up, and a searing pain shot through my stomach. My flesh felt like it was melting away as the fire burned through me. I'd say my screams were heard for miles around.

Once branded, the tree let me go. I landed in a heap on the ground, unable to move.

"You've ten minutes to get as far as you can," King Brian announced as he climbed onto the back of his hound and blew the hunt horn once more.

I lay there, trying to breathe through the pain. I wanted to stay curled up in a ball, but remembering the warning, I scrambled to my feet.

I had ten minutes.

It was pitch black and I had no idea how to get home. I raced through the forest, the trees shooting out their branches, tripping me at every turn. It wasn't long before I heard the horn. Then the sound of howling filled the air. I picked up speed and prayed to every saint I could think of that I'd make it out alive.

"Did you find the exit, Grandpa?" Caitlin asked, completely absorbed in the story.

"I didn't. Not yet," Grandpa said, then hushed her so he could finish his tale. He drained the last of the golden liquid in his glass and relit his pipe.

"Now, where was I?" Grandpa said. He closed his eyes, delving back into his memories once more.

The sound of the hounds galloping was all around me. Every direction I turned, they seemed to be getting closer. The only thing I could do was keep running. I ran through the trees, hoping it would lead me home. What I found was open fields.

The moon was high in the sky, casting a glow across the exposed landscape. There was nowhere to hide. I thought about going back through the forest, but before I could turn around, I heard growling right behind me. I stopped and listened for any movement. I swear I felt the warm breath of that beast against the back of my legs.

When I turned around, Prince Diarmuid and his men were right behind me.

"He's mine," Diarmuid said as he dug his feet into the back of the thing he was riding.

I don't know how to describe it. It wasn't a dog, or a wolf, or anything I'd seen before. This was a large black hairy creature, almost as tall as me, with huge green eyes and deadly sharp teeth. It looked like it wanted to eat me whole. It swiped at me, catching my arm with its claws as it tore away my shirt sleeve. It ripped through my skin like it was paper.

"Now, now, Bran," Diarmuid said. "Give him a chance. It's no fun if we can't chase him."

The beast lowered his head and whined.

"Run," Diarmuid shouted at me. "I'll give you a head start."

I just stood there, shocked. My stomach burned and my arm was slashed, with blood dripping all over the place. They wanted me to run so they could chase me.

With open fields behind me, and a horde of beasts in front of me, I didn't have a choice. I turned towards the fields and pumped my legs as hard as I could. I ran straight, but it was open country as far as my eyes could see. I knew within seconds the hounds would be on top of me. I veered to the left and raced ahead. The growling noise behind me was getting louder.

I dared a quick look.

Prince Diarmuid was leading the hunt. And at the speed they were moving, I'd be caught in under a minute.

The forest was coming into sight, so I willed my aching body to get me there. The hounds were gaining ground with every step I took, but I made it and ducked behind the trees, hoping they'd ride straight past.

They stopped dead in front of the forest and began circling the area.

"You can't hide," Diarmuid shouted. "The brand is a beacon. It tells me exactly where you are, Michael O'Riordan. Come out now, or I'm sending the hounds in for you."

My mind was battling to make sense of it all. I didn't move—I *couldn't* move. There was no escape. I was going to be eaten alive. In a last-ditch attempt to save myself, I clambered up the tree. I thought if I could get high enough, I might be able to see a way out. I was about halfway up when the tree started moving.

The branches shot out everywhere, trying to knock me to the ground. I hung on for dear life, my arms and legs wrapped around a branch. Another branch coiled around my leg, ripping me from the tree.

Once more, I hung upside down, facing death.

The tree was alive. Its fierce eyes staring at me as it grinned.

Without warning, the tree pulled its branch back and hurled me through the air. Prince Diarmuid jumped from his hound at the same time, catching hold of my trouser leg. I flew, like a missile, Prince Diarmuid in tow.

In those few seconds, I prepared myself for death. I made peace with the fact that I'd been so stupid and that I'd never see my sweet Sheila again.

As my body plummeted, I closed my eyes, not wanting to see the ground rise to meet me. The thumping sound in my ears was my only company.

I landed with a splash.

The unexpected, freezing water caused me to panic. My arms flapped frantically as I tried to reach the surface. As my head escaped the water, my lungs filled with the biggest breath I've ever taken. I was still here, still alive. For a split second, exhilaration took over.

I wasn't above water for long, though.

Diarmuid, the nasty bugger, was dragging me down as he tried to climb up my body. My head sunk below the water, but my feet could touch the bottom. I'd heard leprechauns couldn't swim. And as I remembered this, an idea formed in my mind. I reached out and pulled him up to the surface, keeping his head above the water while I looked around. There was no sign of a shoreline or bank of any sort.

"Where are we?" I asked Diarmuid, who was still coughing and spluttering.

His face was as white as a ghost.

"Get me out of here, Michael O'Riordan!" he shouted. "I can't swim!"

"Can ya not?" I said as I loosened my grip, letting him sink just a little.

His eyes widened in fear. "Please, get me out of here!"

"What's in it for me?" I asked.

"I'll free you from the hunt, show you the way out of Faery," he said. "Just get me out of the water!"

"Do I have your word on that, your highness?" I asked, letting his head dip below the water before pulling him up again.

"You do, you do!" he said.

"Say the words, the sacred oath," I demanded.

"I, Diarmuid, Prince of the clan of Tuatha, hereby solemnly swear that on return to land, I will free Michael O'Riordan from the binds of the hunt and take him to the exit of Faery."

Leprechauns may well be nasty little buggers, but they kept their word. A promise from a leprechaun was sacred. Their word was oath.

"Happy now?" Prince Diarmuid said in between spitting out mouthfuls of water.

"I am," I said as I stood up.

The water wasn't very deep, just up past my chest. But Diarmuid didn't know that, and as I waded through the shallow water to find the bank, he cursed and swore at me.

"You tricked me, you blaggard!" Diarmuid shouted at me. "You'll pay for this, Michael O'Riordan."

"I can always drop you," I said, dipping him deep into the water. He shook his head and remained quiet till we found dry land.

When we reached the bank, King Brian and the rest of the hunt were waiting.

"Your majesty," I said with a bow. Then I gently placed Diarmuid on the ground.

"You did a good thing, Michael O'Riordan," King Brian said. "You didn't have to. You could have let my son drown. Thank you."

"No thanks necessary," I said with a smirk. "Diarmuid here made a sacred oath. He promised to return me home and free me from the hunt."

"And it shall be honoured," King Brian said.

"Father, wait," Diarmuid interrupted.

"Did you not speak the sacred oath?" King Brian asked, turning to Diarmuid.

"I did, Father," he said, bowing his head.

"Then it shall be fulfilled. Michael O'Riordan, I release you from the hunt. The veil has been lifted and you may return home," King Brian announced.

I watched as the air in front of me shimmered. I felt my stomach tingle. Lifting my shirt up, I watched in awe as the brand vanished.

I climbed out of the water and bowed. "Thank you, your highness." Then I ran straight ahead.

In a blink, I was back on Sliabh Na Chullaigh. I bent down, placing my hands on my knees as I took in a deep breath. It was over. I was home.

I turned to where the veil was and smiled. "Not as stupid as I look, hey, Diarmuid?" I whispered into the night air.

Suddenly the air rippled and King Brian was standing in front of me.

"Thought you could fool us, did you, Michael O'Riordan? You thought wrong," he said. "You may not be part of tonight's hunt, and you may be home, but there is punishment for your trickery. Should you or any of your children ever set foot on Irish soil when the full moon shines, you will be hunted down. Diarmuid's oath stands. You are free to go. But remember my warning, Michael. You are branded for life. And should your children be born on Irish soil, they too will be branded."

With that said, he vanished. A searing pain shot through me, forcing me to the ground. I writhed in agony, feeling as if a hot iron was being held over my stomach. I don't know how long I lay there screaming, but once the pain subsided, the brand was back. And it's been there ever since. It burns every full moon.

Caitlin could hardly get her mind around this incredible story. "And that's why you left Ireland, Grandpa? Because of the curse?"

"Yes, lass," Grandpa said. "I pleaded with Sheila to leave with me the next day, but she refused. Ireland was her home. And so, two weeks later, I packed my bags and boarded a ship bound for America. I've never been home since."

"What about King Brian, Grandpa?" Caitlin asked anxiously. "Did you ever see him again?"

"Oh, I see him all right, the conniving little—" Grandpa stopped and took a deep breath. "I see him every full moon, when he comes to ask if I'm ready to go home and join the hunt."

Caitlin stared at him. "You won't join, will you, Grandpa?"

"I don't know, Caitlin. I'd do anything to visit my home again," Grandpa said. "But it's too dangerous. They're waiting for me, you know. But I will tell you this: If I could find a way to kill him, I'd be home in a shot. Your grandma would love it. The green fields, the smell of the countryside—do her the world of good, it would."

"I'm sorry, Grandpa," Caitlin said as she watched his face fall.

"Don't be, lass. It was a long time ago, now. And I don't regret my life here one bit," Grandpa told her, patting her knee. "I met your grandma, and sure I wouldn't have it any other way. Now let's go and see if your mother has dinner ready."

As Grandpa rose from his chair, he let out a moan. He bent over, gripping his stomach.

"What's the matter, Grandpa?" Caitlin said, rushing to his side.

"It's just the brand," he said. "Tonight's a full moon."

Caitlin was sure her grandpa made up the story. It was Halloween, after all. But he hadn't smiled, not even once during the telling of his time in Faery. His face had been so serious, telling her about Diarmuid, King Brian and those awful hounds. And when it came to the part about never being able to return to his beloved Ireland, he looked heartbroken.

Still, it was just a story.

"Look," Grandpa said, lifting his shirt.

Caitlin stared at the scarred skin. It was glowing red. Then it changed shape. Right there across his stomach, clearly visible, was the face of a fierce beast with a crown on its head.

"Oh, Grandpa," Caitlin said, placing her hand over her mouth.

"Don't fret, lass," he said, patting her head. "All you must do is never set foot on Irish soil, love. Then you'll be safe. Now come on, let's get dinner."

They made their way into the kitchen. Mom frowned when she saw them.

"You okay, Dad?" Mary asked.

"Yes, love. Just me scar playing up."

"Well, sit yourself down. Dinner's ready. Caitlin, will you help me with the plates?"

"Sure, Mom."

"Did he tell you the story of the hunt?" her mom asked.

Caitlin nodded.

"Well, don't believe everything you hear."

"But, I *saw* it Mom," Caitlin said. "I saw the brand."

"It's just a story, Caitlin."

They all enjoyed dinner, and later that night when everyone was sound asleep, Caitlin heard her grandpa mumbling. Sneaking down the hall, she stopped outside his bedroom door. With her ear against the door, she heard him talking. There was someone else in the room with him.

"No, not this time, your majesty," Grandpa said quietly. "I won't be joining the hunt."

"What a pity, Michael O'Riordan. I'm not getting any younger, you know," a strange voice said. "I'm still waiting to repay you for your kindness to my son."

"Aye, well, you'll be waiting," Grandpa said.

"Maybe," the other voice said. After a pause, he said, "Your granddaughter is outside, listening. Shall we invite her to join the hunt?"

Caitlin jumped away from the door. But she could still hear the voice from inside.

"Hello, Caitlin," said King Brian. "Do come and join us."

Caitlin raced back to her bedroom, got into bed and pulled the covers up tight. Grandpa's story went around and around in her head. She was convinced she could hear some kind of animal growling outside her door.

"It's just a story," Caitlin whispered. "Not real, only a story."

Then she remembered something she'd overheard a few weeks ago. It was a conversation between her Mom and Dad. They were planning a special surprise for Grandpa for his birthday…a family trip to Ireland.

THE END

The Mirror

Ann was looking at herself in the mirror. It was an old-style vanity set—an antique, with a great big mirror that tilted. It had lots of drawers and secret compartments to hide jewelry.

The mirror used to be Grandma's, but now belonged to her. She was so engrossed, she didn't hear her mom coming up the stairs.

"Do you ever move away from that mirror, Ann?" Mom asked, startling her. She was standing in the bedroom doorway.

"I have group photos on Friday," Ann said, without taking her eyes from her reflection in the mirror. "I want to look good, is all."

"Yes, well, you need to perfect your timing too," Mom said. "You're going to be late for school."

"Sorry, Mom," Ann said, jumping up and grabbing her backpack.

Friday was the annual cheerleaders group photos and Ann was determined to look her best. She hated photos, but this year something changed. This year, she wanted to wipe the smile off Clare Johnson's face.

Clare got on her nerves, always the best at everything. The perfect figure, the perfect hair, the perfect clothes, and she knew it too. They'd been good friends once, but that all changed when they reached high school. Clare decided Ann wasn't cool enough anymore.

"You dress like you're still in fifth grade," Clare said after the first week. "I want to be noticed."

Ann tried, but after a month she gave up. She didn't like the person Clare was becoming. Clare would do anything to be popular, even rejecting her best friend.

When they both made the cheerleading squad, things got worse. Clare made a point of laughing at every wrong move Ann made. And as Clare's popularity increased, so did the jeering. Ann tried to shrug it off because she loved cheerleading.

Last year's photos were a disaster. Clare shoved Ann out of the photo at the last minute, and she fell face first onto the football field. Everyone laughed. Even the photographer grinned. Ann cried all evening, and even thought about quitting the squad. But she couldn't let Clare win.

"Bullies," her grandmother had said, "are always insecure and jealous people. Never let them get to you. If you show them they're winning at all, they'll never stop."

She knew her grandmother was right, but it still hurt. She made her way to school—in a rush, as usual—and conjured up images of the photoshoot and how she would look amazing in all the photos. It was the only thing that kept her going. She'd spent all her allowance on new makeup, then spent the entire week practicing new techniques in the mirror.

"Only two days to go," Ann thought. "Then I'll show Clare."

Ann didn't see the car pulling into the parking lot as she stepped off the pavement. The horn made her jump.

"Still blind as ever, I see," Clare said, walking past. She giggled with all her friends.

Ann hadn't even realized the girls were behind her. She'd been too busy imagining her perfect photographs. And now she'd given them something else to jeer her about. She felt the tears sting her eyes, but she refused to cry. She could still hear them laughing as she made her way through the school doors. They laughed all the way to their lockers.

"Two more days," Ann said quietly. "Then I'll show them. They'll finally notice me."

The day passed without further incident. But cheerleading practice was cancelled due to some issue with Coach Peters. Ann was disappointed, but it meant she had more time to perfect her image for the photos on Friday.

As she sat on the stool beside her vanity unit, she inspected her face. Her mom always told her she was beautiful, but moms always say that kind of stuff.

She studied her features carefully. Her skin was clear and her cheeks had a slight blush. Her mom said they were cute, but Ann didn't want rosy red cheeks. She wanted a flawless complexion. Her strawberry blonde hair came down in waves—not straight, not curly. It hung down her back, and it was the thing she loved most.

Her eyes were a bright blue, and really stood out with mascara and eyeliner. She smiled in the mirror, trying her best to look confident. She failed miserably, then scowled at her reflection.

She tried again, placing her hand under her chin, like she'd seen in magazines and online tutorials. No matter what she did, it still didn't look right.

"This is useless," she said, pushing back from the vanity unit. "I'll never fit in."

She shoved her makeup to one side and bent down to pick up her backpack. "I might as well start my homework. At least that's something I can do right."

Ann was a straight A student. And as much as she loved books and learning, it didn't help her popularity status.

Something in the mirror moved.

Ann turned around in her chair. She looked around her messy room, but there was nothing unusual. Turning back to the mirror, she noticed it was there again.

Ann stared at the mirror.

There was a grey shadow over her left shoulder. She placed her hand on her shoulder, watching closely in the mirror. The shadow moved to her right shoulder. Ann turned, but there was nothing there. Her bedroom was still empty—silent, except for her accelerated breathing. When she turned her attention back to the mirror, the shadow was gone.

"Great," Ann said quietly. "Now I'm imagining things."

She shook her head and laughed, but it took a while to calm her breathing down. She worked on her homework, but she couldn't shake the feeling that someone was watching her. And that someone was *in* the mirror. She found herself checking the mirror every couple of minutes, but the shadow never reappeared.

Around 5:30, Mom called up to her.

A little spooked, and with her homework only halfway finished, she closed her books and went downstairs for dinner.

"How's the posing coming along?" Mom asked during dinner.

"It's not," Ann said.

"You'll look beautiful as always," her mom said, placing her hand on Ann's head.

"Thanks, Mom," Ann said. "I'm going to finish my homework."

"Don't stay up too late," her mom called.

Ann decided to try out one of the new makeup techniques she'd seen before she took a shower. It was a new "smoky eye" effect, and it looked stunning on the girl in the YouTube video. Arranging all her makeup on her desk, Ann pulled up the video on her phone. She watched it through, then set it to the start again so she could follow along.

Everything was going well until it came to blending and getting the eyeshadow into the creases.

"I can't see what I'm doing," Ann said, getting frustrated and moving closer to the mirror. She wished she'd bought the magnifying mirror she'd seen at the mall on Saturday.

Huffing loudly, she gripped the side of the mirror so she had something to hold onto as she moved her face in closer. She picked up the small brush she'd been using and closed one eye.

"That's better," she said, smiling at her reflection.

The lights flickered.

Ann jumped and accidently poked herself in the eye. Her eyes stung as she reached for a tissue. She looked over at the bedside lamp, which had since flickered and gone out.

"Mom? My light bulb is blown," Ann called. "Can you bring me up a new one?"

She dabbed at the tears, drying her eyes so she could fix the mess she'd made. She reached over to adjust the light beside her mirror.

"Not great," Ann said. "But it'll have to do."

Picking up the brush once more, she leaned in close with her face right next to the mirror.

"Just a couple more strokes," she thought, positioning the brush at the corner of her eyelid.

Again, something moved in the mirror.

This time she saw what it was. She watched the dark shadow move across the mirror.

"What was that?" Ann blinked, then rubbed her eyes.

The shadow appeared again.

Ann turned around, scanning her bedroom to see where it went. Her room was empty.

She turned back to the mirror.

The shadow remained.

Doing her best to ignore it, she picked up the tissue she'd been using and wiped the mirror.

"There, that ought to do it," Ann said, enjoying the results.

The shadow was still there.

Ann stared at the dark blob on her mirror. "What is going on? What *is* that?"

Her breath caught as the shadow moved again, then disappeared, leaving only her reflection staring back at her.

Ann shook her head. "I'm losing it." Shrugging it off, she leaned in close to inspect her attempt at "smoky eyes." It wasn't too bad.

Ann smiled.

Her reflection didn't smile back.

Ann watched as her reflection moved closer.

"This can't be happening," she said, moving back from the mirror. "It can't be real."

When she stood up and moved from her chair, eyes wide with fear, her reflection still didn't move.

"Mom!" she screamed, running towards the bedroom door.

"What's all the noise, Ann?" her mother said, pushing the door open. "It took me a few minutes to find where dad put the light bulbs."

"My mirror!" Ann shouted, clearly upset. "There's something wrong with it."

"You and that mirror, Ann," her mom said, shaking her head. "What's wrong with it?"

"I saw something in it."

"Well, yes," her mom said. "That is what usually happens when you look in a mirror. You see things."

"No, Mom. I mean there's something wrong with it," Ann explained. "I smiled, but the *me* in the mirror didn't smile back. I was doing my makeup, practicing for Friday, and then…"

"Enough," her mom said. "I don't want to hear another word about Friday, or the cheerleading photos. You're obsessing, Ann. It's not healthy. If you don't

stop this nonsense, you won't be going. Do you understand?"

Ann nodded.

"Good. Now go and have your shower and get ready for bed," her mom said. She quickly changed the bulb and left the room.

Ann looked at the mirror.

"Okay, okay," she said, forcing herself to get control. "Maybe I am obsessing about Friday a bit."

After showering, she sat in front of the mirror, carefully combing out any tangles. She watched, almost hypnotically, as the brush made its way through her long hair.

"I really do have nice hair," Ann mumbled as she bent to pick up her hairdryer.

As she dried it, something in the mirror caught her attention. A dark figure stood behind her. She looked, but there was nothing there.

"That's it," Ann said. "First thing tomorrow, I am cleaning this mirror."

As soon as she resumed blow-drying her hair, the lights flickered—once, then twice.

The temperature in the room suddenly dropped, causing her to shiver. All the hairs on the back of her arms stood to attention.

Something felt off.

She looked around, her eyes drawn to the mirror.

Instead of a blonde-haired girl, a dark-haired girl stared back. Her hair was long and hung limply around her face. Her eyes were dull and filled with tears.

"You did this, Ann," the girl said. "You let her out. It's all your fault. And now you're next."

Ann rubbed her eyes. She was seeing things. Peeking through her fingers, she looked towards the mirror once more. The girl was still there.

"She's coming to get you, Ann."

Ann rubbed at her arms. The cold was starting to take hold. The lights flickered again.

The girl in the mirror screamed.

Ann covered her ears. Slowly, she turned around, unsure of what to expect.

Her room was empty.

"This is crazy," Ann said. "I must be daydreaming. Either that, or I'm having some kind of nightmare reality."

Ann turned back to the girl in the mirror. The girl's face was pale, her mouth open wide in shock.

"Who are you?" Ann asked. "What do you want?"

"You did this," the girl said. "You woke her. She's coming for you, Ann. You spent too long in front of the mirror, begging to be beautiful, trying so hard to look perfect."

"Who did I wake?" Ann asked, scanning her room.

"Me," a new voice said.

Ann sat paralyzed in the chair. She didn't want to turn around, especially not when a bony hand gripped her shoulder. The fingers were long and thin, like those of an old lady, but they were strong. Ann tried to move her shoulder, loosen the grip, but whoever it was had a firm hold.

"You're mine now, stupid girl," the voice said.

It was scratchy and high-pitched, like the voices Disney uses for evil witches. Ann felt sharp nails dig into her shoulder. Now it was her turn to scream.

"Look up, little girl," the voice said. "Look up and see me."

Ann refused, shaking her head and keeping her eyes trained on the floor.

"Don't do it," the girl in the mirror told her.

"Be quiet, you!" the evil voice roared.

Ann heard the girl in the mirror scream in pain. When she finally lifted her head and looked in the mirror, her stomach turned and tears burned her eyes.

Behind her was the vilest woman she had ever seen. Her long dark hair moved all by itself, as if a strong wind was blowing through it. Her face was grey and stretched out, as if pulled out of shape. Black veins snaked their way through her horrid face, and seemed to be moving, crawling underneath her skin.

Her nose was long and jagged, and long thick hairs

stuck out from her chin. Her eyes were the worst—black holes, cold and dead. She was grinning. Ann could see her greyish black teeth. Many were missing, but those that remained were sharp.

She started laughing, and the horrible cackling sound pierced Ann's ear.

"You're mine now," the grotesque woman said, digging her sharp fingernails further into Ann's delicate skin.

The searing pain of her skin tearing made Ann squirm, but the woman kept laughing.

"Do you think I'm beautiful?" the woman asked.

Ann couldn't move. Her body was frozen and her eyes were fixed to the mirror, which began to glow, first green and then blue.

"Ready for your new home, Ann?" The woman placed her other hand on Ann's back, and pushed.

Reaching out, Ann grabbed the side of her vanity and held on with all her might.

"Stop fighting me, girl!" the woman shrieked, sinking her nails into Ann's hands, forcing her to release her grip.

The woman shoved her again. Ann's head hit the mirror. She felt herself being pulled *inside* the mirror.

"No!" she screamed as darkness swallowed her.

"Ann! Wake up!" her mom shouted.

Ann felt someone shaking her. She bolted upright, trying to figure out where she was.

"Are you okay?" her mom asked. "I heard you screaming. You had me scared to death."

Ann looked around the room in a panic. She'd fallen asleep at her vanity table.

It was all a dream—a nightmare.

"I had a terrible dream about my mirror," Ann said. She cried, wrapping her arms around her mom's waist. "It was awful, Mom. So real."

"You're okay," her mom said, stroking her hair. "It was just a dream. Get into bed, now. It's getting late."

Ann turned and looked at her mirror. Only her reflection stared back.

She reminded herself it was just a dream as she leaned over to turn off her bedside lamp. Snuggling into her duvet, she closed her eyes. Visions of the hideous woman swam in her mind. She couldn't shake the feeling she was being watched. The girl's words echoed in her mind.

Too long in front of the mirror
You woke her
She's coming for you

The words went round and round until Ann finally dozed off. It was restless, broken sleep.

Ann woke feeling tired. After getting washed up and dressed, she took her seat in front of the mirror and placed her makeup in front of her.

"I'll definitely need this today."

She picked up her mascara and raised her eyes to the mirror. A black shadow moved behind her. Her heartrate doubled as fragments of her nightmare returned to her mind.

"I'm beautiful just as I am," Ann said, and stood up. She threw her mascara on the table and walked away.

"Ann?" Her mother could only stare when her daughter entered the kitchen, makeup free. "Honey, you look beautiful."

"Thanks, Mom," Ann said, and smiled. "I don't feel like putting any makeup on today."

Her mom kissed her on the cheek. "You don't need it. True beauty comes from within."

Ann felt great as she left for school. She had plenty of time to enjoy her walk, which was something she'd missed the past year. She'd spent so much time perfecting her look every morning, she practically ran to school every day.

"I've missed this," she said as she strolled along.

School was great. Even Clare smiled at her.

That afternoon, Ann arrived home feeling better than she had all year.

"How was school, darling?" Mom asked.

"Great," Ann said, running up the stairs.

"Oh, by the way, darling," Mom said. "I cleaned your mirror today. There was a horrible stain on it. I don't know what you got on it, but it was a nightmare to get off."

Ann felt a shiver run down her spine. "Thanks,

Mom!" she called, then pushed open the door to her bedroom.

It was freezing inside.

Ann looked around, doing her best to avoid looking at the mirror. She threw her bag beside her bed, and on trembling legs made her way across the room. Quickly, she flipped the mirror over so it faced the wall.

"There," she said, smiling. "I can't see anything."

That awful voice came back.

"You *will* look, Ann," said the woman from her dream.

Ann jumped backwards.

It was her—the woman who tried to shove her into the mirror.

Visions of her nightmare filled her mind as she backed up.

Then she stopped. Without thinking, she picked up her hairbrush.

"Not this time," Ann screamed as she flipped the

mirror over and slammed the brush into it. The glass shattered. "I'll never look at you again."

Satisfied, she went to sit on her bed. Instead of wasting time in front of the mirror, she flipped through her CDs to find some music—something else she loved, but hadn't been doing much of lately because of obsessing with her looks.

"Dinner in five, Ann," her mom called.

"Okay, Mom," Ann called back. "I'll be right down."

She gathered the CDs into a pile and was just about to put them back on her shelf when she heard a knock on the door.

"Mom, I said I'd be down in a minute," Ann said, crossing the room.

But when she opened the door, she froze.

"Ready for your new home?" the woman said.

Nightmare Lady was standing in the hallway.

She was holding up a mirror.

THE END

The Medallion

Bryce was really hoping his dad hadn't seen the road sign.

"What do you think, son?" asked his dad. "Should we go for it?"

"Come on, Dad," Bryce said. "The fun fair?" He groaned as he watched his dad take the exit.

"But you love the fair, son."

"Yeah, when I was nine years old," Bryce said. "I'm not a kid anymore, Dad. I'm almost thirteen."

His dad sighed. "I thought it would be fun. It's the last chance we have to spend time together. You know I'm going to be gone, working overseas for most of this year."

A wave of guilt washed over him. Bryce knew his dad was trying, and here he was being a pain. This was the last day they'd get to spend together for quite some time. His dad would be travelling to America on Monday, and he could be gone for the whole year.

Realizing what a jerk he was being, Bryce turned to face his dad. "Okay, we can go to the fun fair. But no kiddie rides."

His dad grinned. "Sure thing. But what about the bumper cars? You still like those, don't you?"

Bryce laughed. "Yeah, Dad, I do."

He relaxed and decided to enjoy the day. It didn't matter where they went. The whole point of their day out was to spend time together, and Bryce was determined to make the most of it.

The fair was crowded.

Tourists were snapping pictures, and the sounds of laughter and screaming kids filled the air. The unmistakable scent of popcorn and cotton candy caused another big grin as he breathed in deeply. Bryce remembered all the times they'd come to the fair. How his dad had won the ring toss and the shootouts on every occasion. Bryce always brought home the best prizes.

"Where to first?" his dad asked, pulling him from his memories.

"I'm not sure. How about we just walk around first," Bryce said. "Let's see if there's anything new. Then we can do the shootout. I bet I can beat you this year."

His dad laughed. "I don't know about that, son, but you can try."

They strolled through the fair, stopping to look at all the different stalls that caught their attention.

His dad held up a silk scarf. "Do you think your mom will like this one?"

"Dad, that's the tenth time you've asked me that," Bryce told him. "I'm sure she'd like them all. What are you looking for?"

"I don't know," Dad said with a shrug. "I wanted to get her something nice, something to remind her of me while I'm gone."

The mood changed as they both thought of what the next year held.

"That one's perfect," Bryce said, breaking the silence. "Get it and let's go to the shootouts. I know I'm going to beat you."

It worked.

His dad paid for the scarf and off they went. Bryce didn't win any of the shootouts, but they had fun and plenty of laughs to go with it. Bryce laughed so much he had a pain in his stomach.

"Are you ready for something to eat?" Dad pointed in the direction of a hot dog vendor.

"Sure, I'm starving," Bryce said, picking up the pace. "We can have a walk around while we're eating, then maybe the bumper cars. What do you think, Dad?"

"Sounds perfect, son," his dad said, draping his arm around Bryce's shoulders.

They both got a hot dog with the works and went back to shopping, making their way from stall to stall. This was one of Bryce's favorite things to do. When he was younger, he used to badger his parents into buying him all sorts of things. This year he was content to look, knowing that the time with his dad was more important. He didn't want him to have to work away for the next year, but there was nothing he could do.

The company his dad worked for was opening a new office in New York, and if his dad didn't go to help set it up, his job would be at stake. It was only a year, and his dad promised he'd come home as often as he could.

"Hey, Bryce, look at these," Dad said. "Didn't you used to collect them?"

Bryce looked up. His dad was standing in front of a stall filled with medallions and gold coins. He moved closer to get a better look.

Browsing through the coin collection, a medallion at the back of the stall caught his eye. "Look, Dad, it's an ouroboros," Bryce said. "You know, the Auryn symbol from The Neverending Story. I loved that movie."

"I remember," his dad said, grinning. "Mom and I must have seen it a thousand times. You wouldn't watch anything else."

"Can I help you?" a woman asked, appearing from behind a pile of scarves and clothes.

Bryce looked up to see a small gypsy lady standing in front of them. She wore a colourful scarf wrapped around her head, and big hoop earrings. Rings covered her fingers and bracelets snaked up her arms.

"Can we see the medallion in the back?" Dad asked. "The one with the snake eating its tail."

"Ah, the ouroboros," said the woman. "It can show your heart's desire." She looked right at Bryce.

The gypsy picked up the medallion and handed it to him. She gave him the creeps, but he reached out to take it. She grinned, and that's when he noticed her rotten teeth, half of them missing.

"Hold it in your left hand," said the old gypsy woman, "and you'll see your true love."

His dad laughed. Bryce pretended not to be embarrassed.

"Oh, go on, son. What harm can it do?"

Bryce cringed and took the medallion. The moment he held it in his left hand, an image of Stephanie Peters entered his mind. She was a girl from school—one that he dreamed about quite often. But this was more than a daydream. More like a vision, the way she was reaching out to him.

Bryce snapped out of it when the gypsy woman placed her old, bony hand on top of his.

"Place it under your pillow at night to dream of your destiny," she said, nodding at Bryce.

"How much?" his dad asked, pulling some cash from his wallet.

"A gift for the boy," she said, refusing the money.

Bryce smiled and shoved the medallion into his pocket. "Come on, Dad, let's go on the bumper cars before it gets too late."

"Thank you," his dad said to the gypsy before turning to leave.

"Don't forget," she called. "Place it under your pillow to see your destiny."

Bryce turned to look at her, but she was gone. An old man was standing behind the stall instead. He shook his head and continued walking.

They went on the bumper cars twice. After that, they ate popcorn, drank soda, and bought some cotton candy for the ride home. It had been a great day.

Bryce was glad his dad had surprised him with a trip to the fair. If he'd had to choose, they would have ended up at the movies. This was a much better idea.

His mom was waiting to hear all about their day. She laughed when Bryce relayed what the gypsy had told him.

"So," she said with a wink. "Did you see your true love when you held it?"

Bryce just laughed it off. He didn't want to talk about girls with his mom. She just laughed and continued the conversation, asking about how their day went.

As a family, they shared what would be their last meal together for a long time. Bedtime came much too soon, though it had been a long, fun day.

Upstairs in his bedroom, Bryce took the medallion from his pocket and placed it under his pillow. He was looking forward to dreaming of Stephanie. He fell asleep quickly, and eased into dreamland.

He found himself standing in a field.

The grass was so long he could touch the tips of it with his fingers. In the distance was a long row of trees, leading to a dense forest. Someone was standing in front of it.

"Stephanie," he whispered as his eyes zoomed in on her.

She giggled and ran into the forest.

Bryce chased after her, but soon became lost. No matter which way he turned, he was surrounded by a thick covering of trees. Tall, menacing trees that whispered in the wind and made him shiver. He heard Stephanie giggle again. When he looked to his right, no one was there.

The trees blocked out the light, allowing only small beams to break through and cast strange shadows on the ground.

"Stephanie! Where are you?" Bryce shouted.

"Over here, Bryce."

He turned in the direction of her voice and started walking. The forest was nearly impossible to get through, and getting worse with each step. Branches scratched at his face as he moved along, travelling deeper into the woods.

"Wait for me!" Bryce hollered in the darkness.

"Hurry up," she called back. Then he heard her laughing.

"Why a forest?" Bryce thought. "Why couldn't we be at the beach? Somewhere it's nice and sunny."

Bryce ran to catch up, but fell to the ground when a branch caught his foot. His hands and knees were covered in dirt. He wiped them on his sweater, then pushed himself up.

The light was growing weaker by the second, making it difficult to see where he was going. The trees swayed in a harsh wind that came out of nowhere.

Soon the noise of their movements grew louder. Shadows played tricks on the forest floor.

Bryce stood still, scanning the area. He cupped his hands in front of his mouth, calling out to Stephanie. She was nowhere to be seen, but he heard her laughter coming from up ahead.

He pushed the sense of fear down and willed his legs to move. Moving forward, all he could do was follow the sound of Stephanie's voice.

"Over here, Bryce," she called.

Moving in her direction, something brushed off his face. It wasn't a branch, but something soft and sticky—like cobwebs. His hands immediately wiped at his face. He hated spiders.

"I can't find you, Stephanie," he shouted. "You'll have to come back for me."

Her laughter was all he heard.

A foul smell filled the air, worse than any stink bomb the older boys sometimes let off in school.

"What is that smell?" Bryce said, covering his nose.

"Bryce! Where are you, Bryce?"

He relaxed when he heard her voice. "Over here, Stephanie! Beside the tree."

"You sure it's a tree, scared little boy?"

Stephanie's voice sounded different.

Bryce felt for the tree, but jumped away when he felt a pair of hands.

He turned to find Stephanie behind him.

"That wasn't funny," he told her. "You scared me half to death."

"I didn't mean to," she said. "Or did I?"

Bryce blinked and looked at her. Had Stephanie really said that? But it wasn't Stephanie standing there, it was the gypsy woman from the fair. She was grinning at him, just like before.

"Ready to meet your destiny?" the gypsy woman said. She grabbed his arm and pulled him closer. "Master will enjoy you."

"Let me go!" Bryce shouted as he pulled his arm back, wrenching it away from her.

He started to run.

"You can't escape," the gypsy woman shouted.

Bryce raced through the forest, his heart thumping loudly in his ears. Behind him, he could hear more laughter. And it was getting closer.

Branches lashed at his face as his feet pounded the ground. He couldn't see where he was going. His foot caught on something and he tumbled to the forest floor. He scrambled through the filth on his hands and knees, clawing his way forward.

"I have to get out of here," Bryce thought.

"It's too late," the gypsy said. "He's here."

"Oh, God," Bryce said, trying to get to his feet.

The smell was getting worse. It was so bad it made his head hurt.

A dreadful moan filled the air.

There was movement from all sides. Shadows played awful tricks on his eyes. Fog swept in and curled around his feet.

"Here he is, Master," said the gypsy. Her voice was on top of him now. "All fresh and ready."

Bryce closed his eyes and prayed for someone to rescue him.

"Well done, Norma," a deep voice said.

Bryce forced himself to look. When he opened his eyes, he looked around in absolute shock.

There was no one there.

No gypsy.

No Master.

Shaking his head, he started to lift himself off the ground, but his feet were held firm. He pulled at his legs, but nothing.

A cold chill blew across his face, bringing with it the putrid sewer smell from before. Cold sweat broke out on his forehead as he looked around, waiting for *them* to come out of the darkness.

"I have to get out of here," Bryce whispered to himself. He tugged at his legs once more, but it was useless.

"You won't escape," a voice whispered in his ear.

Bryce jumped. "Who's there?"

"Your own personal nightmare," the voice whispered in his other ear.

"Yes, a nightmare," Bryce thought. "This is only a dream." All he had to do was wake up. Gripping the skin on his forearm, Bryce squeezed with all his might.

"AHH!" Bryce cried out in pain.

Opening his eyes slowly, he expected to find himself back in his bedroom. But he was still trapped in the creepy forest.

"That didn't work, did it?" said the nightmare voice. Then it laughed at him. "Want to try again?"

"You're not real. This isn't real," Bryce shouted. "It's a stupid dream. A terrible nightmare, that's all."

"You sure about that?" the voice asked, running its cold hand down Bryce's cheek.

Bryce shook with fear, ready to beg for his life. Tears filled his eyes as he grabbed desperately at his legs.

"Leave me alone!" Bryce shouted into the darkness.

"Oh, but I can't do that, Bryce," the voice said. "I'm part of you, now."

The voice was everywhere—in front, behind, all around him.

"It's just a voice," Bryce thought. "There's nothing really there. It's all a dream. I'm going to wake up any minute now."

He cringed when he heard more laughter.

Please don't let anything be there...

Please don't let anything be there...

Bryce closed his eyes, repeating his mantra. Slowly, he opened his eyes, preparing for the worst. Air puffed from his mouth as he sighed in relief. The forest was empty.

"Looking for me?"

Bryce screamed.

There was a face right in front of him. So close that their noses were almost touching. He couldn't look away. His eyes were wide as he stared into the eyes of what was in front of him.

"Thought I wasn't real, did you?" the nightmare voice said. "Come here. Let me smell you, boy."

Two bony hands reached out and pulled him closer as a long pointed nose sniffed at him.

"Nearly there," the voice said with a laugh. He turned his head, still holding Bryce tightly in his grip.

"You know what to do," he shouted.

Bryce heard a rustling sound. Then movement. There was something else out there. Things were moving in all directions. He heard the leaves rustling on the ground all around him. Closer and closer they came—whatever they were.

Bryce wriggled and squirmed. "Let me go!"

"Oh, it's not time yet. You don't smell scared enough."

Bryce kicked out with his feet. They were no longer stuck. They were no longer pinned to the ground. He heard a screech, then more scurrying.

"Come on, you lot," the voice said. "You can do better than that."

Laughter, screams, and moans came from every direction as Bryce struggled to release himself from the creature's grip.

"Stop!" the voice roared.

Bryce's body stiffened. He couldn't move or speak.

"That's better," the creature said, sniffing the air around Bryce's body. "Now, where shall I begin? Which part of you will taste the best? Shall we see how you handle…pain."

All around Bryce, creatures appeared. Black shapes, each as big as a fist, were all moving towards him. He sensed movement on his legs, but couldn't see what it was. A tickling sensation began at his ankles as…*things* began crawling up his legs.

"Please don't be spiders," Bryce cried.

Just thinking about them crawling up his body caused his breathing to come in short bursts. He was practically hyperventilating.

His eyes grew wide as the biting began. Quick, stabbing pains at first, then gradually getting worse, much more painful with each tiny nip of flesh.

The creature came up close, right into Bryce's face. It grinned at him, showing off a mouthful of huge, discoloured, jagged teeth. A long, clawed finger reached out and moved the hair away from Bryce's face.

"Nice and sweaty now," the creature said, moving the clawed finger back and forth. "Keep going, my little darlings. That's it—higher, right up to his handsome little face, which you may devour."

Bryce felt the spiders—or whatever they were—crawling up his body, exploring, biting as they went.

Without warning, the creature dragged his claw across Bryce's forehead, tearing it open. The scream that wanted to rip from his throat was trapped, and he remained silent. He watched as the creature brought the claw to his lips. Then a long tongue came sweeping out to taste the blood.

"Perfect," the creature said.

Bryce tried one last time to move, to wrench himself free. Dark hands appeared from every direction, gripping at his clothes. He tried to move, to squirm and duck out of their reach, but whatever the creature had done to him had rendered him motionless.

He couldn't take it anymore. Blood poured down his forehead, mixing with the tears that spilled from his eyes.

The spiders continued biting at his legs, arms, chest, and everywhere else. And the creature in front of him was coming back for another taste.

"Almost there," the creature said with a laugh. Then he sniffed the air. "It's almost time."

"Time for what?" Bryce managed to ask.

"Time to become one of us, boy," the creature said. Then he lunged forward, sinking his sharp fangs into Bryce's neck.

Bryce screamed.

The sound that ripped from his throat was so loud that it woke him from his nightmare. It also woke the entire house.

The creature's face, so fresh in his mind, appeared to still be standing in front of him as he leapt out of bed. He scrubbed at his legs to make sure there were no spiders.

Dad came running into the room. "Bryce, are you okay?"

He turned, wide-eyed, to see his dad standing at his bedroom door.

"Yeah, I'm okay. I just…" Bryce took a few deep breaths. "I just had a bad dream, is all."

"Are you sure you're okay?" Dad asked, coming into the room. "I haven't heard you scream like that since…well, ever."

"I'm fine, Dad. Honestly." Bryce nodded. He touched his neck to make sure there were no bite marks, or holes, or blood on his forehead.

"Well, try and get some sleep, okay?" Dad said as he patted his son's sweat-soaked head. "See you in the morning."

"Goodnight, Dad."

Bryce waited until he was alone again. Then he got out of bed and started pacing his bedroom. There was no going back to sleep. Not now. Not after the worst nightmare he'd ever had was still fresh in his mind. He knew that if he dared to close his eyes, he would see that monster again. He shivered just thinking about it.

Bryce checked his watch and saw that it was almost five a.m. Not much longer until morning, so he decided to read and take his mind off the hideous face from his dreams.

At seven, he made his way downstairs. His mom followed shortly after, upbeat and fully rested.

"Morning, Bryce," she said, strolling across the kitchen to put the coffee on.

"Morning, Mom," he said, barely lifting his head from his cereal.

"So, did it work?" Mom asked.

Confused, Bryce looked over at his mom. "Did what work?"

"Your medallion. Did you dream about your true love? Was it that Stephanie girl I've heard you talk about?"

"No," Bryce snapped at her. Then he resumed eating his breakfast. He felt bad about snapping at his mom like that. It wasn't her fault. And besides, he was glad to see her so cheery in the morning.

"I'm sorry, Mom," Bryce said. "I didn't mean to snap. I'm a little tired this morning. Didn't sleep well."

"That's okay," Mom said, ruffling his hair. "We all have off days."

Bryce finished his breakfast, then headed back upstairs. His mom's question about his dreams stuck in his mind as he made his way to his bedroom. He shoved the pillow off his bed.

There it was—the ouroboros symbol.

Bryce leaned over and picked it up, studying the snake eating its own tail.

"You're mine now, boy," the creature whispered. "I'll see you tonight."

The vision of those ugly, jagged teeth lunging towards him exploded in his mind. He dropped the medallion, trying to shake the images from his head.

The medallion lay flat on the floor. He didn't want the evil relic in the house, but he refused to touch it. Using a shirt from the laundry basket, he scooped it up.

Holding it tightly, he raced down the stairs and out the back door. He lifted the lid of the trash bin.

"That's the last time I try to see my destiny," Bryce said. "No more dreams of Stephanie Peters, either."

The medallion fell to its resting place in the bin.

"In fact, I think I'll stay away from girls altogether," Bryce said as he made his way back inside.

Moments later, the trash man arrived. As he moved the bin, the lid lifted. Seeing the medallion, right on the top of the rubbish, he reached in to retrieve it.

"This looks nice," he thought. Then he wiped it off on his shirt and stuck it in his pocket. "I'm sure Stephanie will love this."

THE END

Campfire Tales

The warm glow of the campfire did nothing to still the tension in Melissa's body. She sat on one of the big old dead trees that surrounded the campfire, waiting anxiously to see what would happen.

It was her first trip away with the Girl Guides, so she had no idea what to expect. The giggles and screeches of the other girls, along with their whispers and stares, caused her heartrate to spike.

"Don't worry about it," said Ava, the girl who'd quickly become her friend on this trip. "It's great fun, you'll see."

The camp leader, Mrs. O'Brien, hushed everyone. She was an older lady, her blonde hair cut short with bits of grey showing through. She wore black-rimmed glasses that she constantly pushed up her nose, or pulled down to glare at the girls if they got out of line.

Mrs. O'Brien wore her Girl Guides uniform with pride—not a wrinkle in sight. She exuded authority. And right now, she stood in the center of the group.

"Okay girls, you all know how this goes," said Mrs. O'Brien, "but I will run through the rules one more time, so that Melissa knows what to do."

Melissa heard a few groans as Mrs. O'Brien held up a book.

"This is the book of ghost stories that has been handed around the campfire since I was a Girl Guide," said Mrs. O'Brien. "When the book is passed to you, it's your turn to tell a scary story. The best stories will be added to this book at the end of camp. It's a great privilege, you know." She ran her hands over the cover of the book. "And remember girls, it doesn't have to be long. Short and sweet is perfectly fine." Then she looked at Carol Johnson, who just shrugged her shoulders.

"Who'd like to go first?" Mrs. O'Brien asked.

Hands flew into the air and the shouts of "Me!" and "I will!" vibrated in Melissa's ears. She wasn't looking forward to this. Ghost stories freaked her out. And telling them around a campfire, in the dark, did not help.

"Okay, Madison, how about you start," said Mrs. O'Brien. "When you're done, please pass the book to the left, going around clockwise and ending with Olivia."

After she placed another log on the fire, Mrs. O'Brien took a seat in her lawn chair. Everyone else had to sit on the fallen trees that had been there forever.

Madison grinned as she took the book.

"Everyone ready to be freaked out?" she asked, followed by what Melissa could only assume was supposed to be a wicked laugh. It sounded more like an excited girly screech.

Madison began her story. It was about a girl who was afraid of the dark getting trapped in a cellar. It was horribly lame, and when the ending came, there were moans and groans from the other girls. She passed the book to Nesa, and the stories continued.

Nesa told the tale of a doll coming to life and terrorizing any child it belonged to.

Melissa started to relax. "It's not as bad as I thought," she whispered to Ava. "The stories aren't too scary. I thought they'd be much worse."

"Yep, pretty lame," Ava whispered back, before Mrs. O'Brien hushed them.

Melissa lowered her head, embarrassed, and continued to listen.

There were twelve girls in her troop. Everyone was seated in a circle around the campfire, roasting marshmallows, making S'mores, and listening to silly ghost stories.

As the book got closer, Melissa's anxiety grew.

"What am I going to say?" she thought. "I don't know any ghost stories?" She didn't want the girls to laugh at her or make fun of her.

"Don't panic. And remember to breathe." She heard her mom's voice whisper in her head. *"You can do it."* This was her mom's speech whenever there was anything worrying her.

Melissa took a deep breath and listened to the stories. There was a story about a nightmare demon, a haunted house, and one about a boy spending an hour in a haunted graveyard.

Melissa thought of what she might say. She could

mix-and-match all the scary stories she'd heard so far, and maybe combine them.

"No, that won't work," Melissa thought. "I need something real."

Her heart pounded in her chest as she clambered for ideas. The book was getting closer, and so was her turn. She imagined being afraid, terrified, and what would cause her to feel that way.

A shadow moved across the campfire.

Melissa had always seen shadows. Most people do, but not like this. She saw them all the time, usually out of the corner of her eye. When she would turn to look, they would vanish. Her body temperature would drop when the shadows came near. Her breath would become a mist leaving her body.

Lost in thought, Melissa didn't notice everything around her begin to fade. When she looked up, the girls, the campfire, even Mrs. O'Brien had all become a haze. Nothing more than a blurry background.

Melissa shook her head and pinched her eyes closed. When she opened her eyes again, nothing had changed. Sounds were all around her, but muffled and hard to understand. Then came the familiar chill that seeped into her body. Her breath became visible in the cold air.

"Melissa."

She heard her name being whispered, so naturally turned to Ava, who was sitting beside her.

Ava was gone. All the other girls had also disappeared. The campfire, blurry but still visible, cast a soft glow on her surroundings.

"Melissa," said the voice again.

A girl's voice, but not from her troop.

"This isn't funny," Melissa said.

Nothing but silence.

"Help me," came the voice again.

It sounded like it was coming from behind her.

Melissa took several deep breaths. "It's not real."

The breeze that had been blowing all evening was

suddenly gone. She shivered and pulled her blanket tighter. Her hands were shaking.

"This isn't funny anymore," Melissa said. She knew the girls played tricks on new members, but this was taking it too far. And how did they know about the shadows? She hadn't told anyone.

"Okay, you guys—joke's over," Melissa said, watching as her breath turned to mist. She knew what it meant. That she was having one of her "episodes." That's what her doctors called them. The real term was psychotic delusion, but her mom felt that was too harsh.

"Melissa," the voice whispered.

This time it was right beside her.

Melissa cringed when something brushed against her. A scream threatened to shatter the silence, but she held it back. She knew her delusions were all in her mind.

In reality, she was sitting around a campfire with the other Girl Guides, and Mrs. O'Brien.

"Stay calm. Don't scream." Melissa repeated these words in her mind. When she looked to her left, then her right, nothing was there.

She relaxed.

"Help me."

The voice came again. Melissa noticed something moving out of the corner of her eye.

She swung around, not wanting it to disappear, whatever it was. Her eyes widened as she saw the outline of a girl.

Melissa's hand flew to her mouth.

"Don't scream," the ghost said. "Please, don't scream. I'm not here to harm you, I promise."

The ghostly figure floated towards her.

"You see me?"

Melissa nodded her head. Although she was terrified at first, seeing her up close, the girl didn't seem as scary.

"Will you help me?" the ghost asked.

"How?" Melissa whispered. "What do you want me to do?"

"Tell my story."

"What story?" Melissa said. "I'm terrible at stories. All the words get mixed up, and I…"

"I will help you tell the story," the ghost said. "I'll whisper it to you, then you repeat it. People need to know what happened to me. Please."

Feeling a need to help, Melissa agreed.

"Okay. Yes," Melissa told the ghost girl. "When it's my turn, I'll tell your story."

The campfire, the other girls, Mrs. O'Brien, and everything else came back into focus as soon as she agreed.

"You okay, Mel?" Ava asked.

"Yeah, fine," Melissa whispered.

"You're up next. Have you thought of a story?"

"I think so," Melissa said, hoping she was right.

"Girls?" Mrs. O'Brien's stern voice reached their ears, and they settled down.

Kelly Ann finished telling her story. The girls all

clapped, then the book passed hands. It was now Melissa's turn to tell a story.

As she gripped the leather binding, the ghost whispered in her ear. "Are you ready?"

Melissa nodded and cleared her throat. "My story is about a girl who haunts these woods…"

As the ghost spoke to her, Melissa relayed her words.

"It was the summer of 1982. And just like all of us here now, the South West Troop 1007 had gathered for the annual camp out. It was three days into camp when Jennifer Davis disappeared."

All the girls began to whisper.

"My mom would have been at camp that year," Madison said.

Two other girls nodded in agreement.

The camp leader, Mrs. O'Brien, shushed them. "Let Melissa tell her story."

"So, it was day three when Jennifer disappeared," Melissa continued, once everyone had quieted down. She repeated everything the ghost whispered in her ear, word for word. "Her best friend, who'd also been at camp, told everyone that Jennifer had gotten really homesick, and that she'd decided to go home the night before."

"Who was the friend?" Madison asked, interrupting again.

"No name," the ghost said. "Not yet."

Melissa felt ice creep through her veins each time the ghost spoke to her. But as agreed, she went on with the story.

"Jennifer, the girl who disappeared, told her best friend that her parents were picking her up. So no one noticed anything was wrong until the day they all arrived back on the bus. Jennifer's parents were there to meet her, but Jennifer wasn't on the bus. Something terrible happened to her in these woods. The truth is…Jennifer Davis was murdered."

The girls all huddled closer together.

"This is the best story yet," one girl said.

"Keep going," the ghost whispered. "We're almost done with the story."

Melissa took a sip of water from her canteen, then adjusted the blanket around her shoulders. She was freezing, but only she could see her cold breath.

"On the night before Jennifer disappeared," Melissa went on, "she told her best friend about the crush she had on Philip Staunton, and how she was going to ask him to the fall dance when they got back to school."

"Look up!" the ghost whispered. "Look at her face! She knows what's coming next!"

Melissa looked up, but had no idea who she was supposed to be looking at.

The camp leader, Mrs. O'Brien, seemed off. She didn't seem to be enjoying the story at all.

"Okay girls, it's getting late," said Mrs. O'Brien. "We should all get some sleep."

"Awww," the girls said. "But we want to hear the rest of the story."

"Everyone knows Jennifer Davis ran away," Mrs. O'Brien snapped.

"Tell them there's not much left," the ghost whispered. "Please, tell them. I've waited so long for the truth to be told. Please."

"Mrs. O'Brien," Melissa said. "There's only a little bit of the story left. Can we finish it tonight?"

"Please," all the girls asked, begging Mrs. O'Brien to let Melissa go on with the story.

"Fine. Go on, then," said Mrs. O'Brien. "But hurry up."

Melissa, poised and ready, continued.

"Jennifer told her best friend about her crush on Philip. But what she didn't know was that her friend was obsessed with him. That's what led to her murder."

All the girls stared, listening intently. Not one of them was giggling or whispering like they did during the other stories. Even Mrs. O'Brien was paying close attention.

"You see, Jennifer didn't just disappear," Melissa went on. "Her best friend asked to meet her in the woods after lights out, so she could help Jennifer come up with a plan to win Philip's heart. Jennifer agreed, then the two girls left the camp in the dead of night. They walked to the waterfall that was less than half a mile away. They'd been there already on the troop's annual hike. Every troop visited Wonder Falls. As Jennifer talked about Philip, her friend plotted her murder. Jennifer would never have Philip because he was hers."

Melissa stopped.

Images of the two girls standing at the top of the waterfall flowed through her mind. As if her body was being controlled by something else, the story rushed from her mouth.

"Jennifer told her friend about her plan to ask Philip to the fall dance," Melissa went on. "Then she started to dance, pretending to hold Philip in her arms, right there above the waterfall. Her friend became angry. And when Jennifer asked her what was wrong, she snapped. She turned on Jennifer, screaming that Philip was hers, and that she had no right to ask him. Without warning, she lunged forward and shoved Jennifer off the edge of the waterfall."

One girl asked, "Did she die?"

"Yes," Melissa answered.

The entire Southwest Troop was mesmerized by the story, especially since it sounded so familiar.

Melissa's body was paralyzed. She raised her head, eyes staring vacantly at the camp leader, Mrs. O'Brien.

The ghost placed her hand on Melissa's shoulder, and Melissa started speaking in a strange voice.

"The name of the friend, my best friend, the one who murdered me…is DeDe McKenzie."

The ghost removed her hand, and Melissa fell forward. She felt dizzy and lightheaded. All the girls were looking at her.

"Are you okay? Ava asked. "What happened?"

Melissa stared at Mrs. O'Brien. The camp leader

looked like she'd seen a ghost. In a way, she had.

"Thank you," the ghost whispered in Melissa's ear. "I'm free now. The truth has finally been told. There's just one more thing you need to say."

Melissa nodded.

Mrs. O'Brien was standing again, ushering the girls to their tents. "Storytime's over," she said with a quiver in her voice.

"Wait," Melissa shouted. "There's one last part to the story."

The girls all reclaimed their seats, eager to hear the last part of the story.

Mrs. O'Brien remained standing, her eyes locked on Melissa.

"Jennifer's body was never found," Melissa went on. "And her friend DeDe never told a soul what happened that night. She lived with it this whole time. And every year since it happened, she's been coming back here, always fearful that one year Jennifer's remains will be discovered."

All the girls were quiet, their eyes glued to her.

"This is the year she will finally be discovered," Melissa went on. "Jennifer's remains have been at the bottom of the waterfall for all these years. And the person who put her there is right here with us. DeDe doesn't go by that name anymore. Does she?" Melissa asked, meeting Mrs. O'Brien's stare.

"Keep going," the ghost whispered as Melissa's body shook with the cold.

"DeDe changed her name to…"

"Stop," said Mrs. O'Brien, then she lunged at Melissa. "Enough. Storytime is over."

Melissa didn't hear her. The ghost had a firm grip on her shoulder. Melissa's body was no longer her own. Her head raised up and met the eyes of the camp leader.

"Hello, DeDe," Melissa said in a strange voice. "Or should I call you Doris?"

Mrs. O'Brien stumbled backwards. "It can't be. Jennifer, is that you?"

"Yes, DeDe. It's time to tell the truth."

The camp leader crumbled to the ground. Her time was up.

The ghost removed her hands from Melissa, and she regained control over her body.

"Thank you," the ghost said. "I've waited so long for someone like you. You'll never know how grateful I am for your gift. Don't let anyone tell you that you're delusional—you're not."

"But the doctors say…" Melissa began.

"You can communicate with the dead, Melissa," said the ghost. "You can see into the other realm. Do not fear it, for only those who are pure of heart can see you. Be brave, Melissa, you have so much good to do."

Melissa's body trembled as she let those words sink in. She had a gift, not a curse.

Camp ended that night with Mrs. O'Brien confessing to the murder of Jennifer Davis. Melissa never feared the cold, or the mist, or the blurred visions again. She had a gift. And she planned to use it to help those that no longer had a voice.

THE END

The Ghost
Train of Horror

"Come on, David. Don't be a chicken."

David froze, eyes locked on the ride in front of him. The Ghost Train of Horror was the one ride he didn't want to go on.

"I'm not chicken," David said. "I just want to get a drink. You guys go ahead. I'll catch up later."

"Yeah, right," Ethan said. "You're afraid to ride the Ghost Train, aren't you?"

"Chicken!" the boys jeered.

David clenched his fists. "I'm not a chicken."

"Prove it," Ethan said with a smirk.

David was the most popular kid at school, but Ethan saw his chance to dethrone him. If the boys saw how much of a scaredy-cat he was, they'd think twice about following his lead.

"Fine," David said, joining the queue with the others. He knew what Ethan was up to, and wasn't going to let him win. Why they were still friends was anyone's guess. They were always at loggerheads—one trying to outdo the other—but it was normal.

The queue stretched back towards the bumper cars. Lines of excited kids waited to test out the new ride. It was the main attraction at the fair this year, and the only thing being discussed at school.

The outside walls had ghosts and snarling monsters painted all over them. Tons of skeletons hung down around the ride. They looked quite real. The carriage seats looked like they'd been made from bones. Green slime covered them, finishing the look of the frightening ride.

The man in charge looked like a zombie. Ripped clothes hung from his body as he ambled along the walkway, motioning to the children to step aboard. David recoiled as he watched him lurch forward, sometimes shouting towards the kids, trying to scare them and get a reaction.

"Brave enough, boys?" asked the zombie man, interrupting the conversation David and his friends were having.

"'Course we are!" Ethan shouted. "This ride better be worth the money."

David paid no attention to Ethan and the other boys. He was too busy taking everything in.

Two large black doors, easily twelve feet high, led

into the Ghost Train of Horror. His mind was busy conjuring up images of ghosts, demons, monsters, and giant axes and knives slashing victims when they least expected it.

"Looks cool, doesn't it?" Ethan said, nudging him.

"Yeah," David replied, not taking his eyes off the black doors. "Really...cool."

They reached the top of the queue.

"Two to a carriage," zombie man shouted, once it was their turn.

"Great," David said, watching as the boys scrambled to get seats. He was odd man out.

"Looks like you get to ride all by yourself," Ethan said, then laughed.

"More room for me," David sneered back. He wasn't going to let Ethan get the better of him.

He climbed into the last carriage and sat back. The zombie man walked from carriage to carriage, pulling down the bone-shaped bar to lock them in.

"Welcome back, David," he whispered as he leaned in close.

"What did you say?" David asked him.

The man looked at him and smiled. "Enjoy the ride."

Ghostly moans and deafening screams boomed from the speakers surrounding the ride. Then came an evil laugh as the carriages began to move. The wheels were grinding along the tracks, lurching forward. David watched the black doors get closer and closer. His pulse raced as he prepared for the crash. There was no getting out of it now. They were going in.

Ethan and the boys were laughing and joking, pointing at the crowd that had gathered to watch the Ghost Train.

Ethan looked back. "You ready for this?" he asked.

"As ready as you are," David replied.

The carriage picked up speed as the black doors creaked open. David stared straight ahead, but there was nothing to see—not yet.

"Welcome to the Ghost Train of Horror," a loud voice boomed from the overhead speakers. "Will you make it out alive?" It ended with evil laughter.

The voices, the scary noises, the howls from the other kids—it all brought with it memories he thought he'd buried forever. His dad had taken him on his first ever ghost train when he was seven. It had terrified him. That one ride had kept him awake for weeks. He couldn't close his eyes without seeing monsters and ghosts coming at him.

"Oooh, so scary," Ethan said.

As David's carriage passed through the doors, they banged shut. Soft glowing lights popped up everywhere.

David took a deep breath. Quietly, so the boys wouldn't hear, he said, "I can handle this. I can handle this. Don't freak out."

A deep thumping sound echoed throughout the chamber. Music with no melody. The scary kind of music that plays in movies when something bad is going to happen.

The carriage moved slowly onwards.

Skeletons hung from the walls, and wailing hags and witches swayed in front of him. They reminded him of his mom's Halloween decorations.

"This isn't so bad," David thought.

The lights went out.

Then the carriage picked up speed.

"The horror is about to begin," a deep voice shouted. "You are about to suffer your greatest fear, whatever that may be. Fear is different for every boy or girl."

"Yeah, right!" Ethan shouted in front. "This ride's rubbish!"

David sat back in his seat. For now, his breathing was calm, even though it was so dark he couldn't see his hands gripping the bar.

The carriage crept forward, gradually increasing speed. David was slammed against the back of the seat. He heard the boys screaming in delight in front of him.

"Here we go," Ethan shouted.

The loud music thumped and echoed in the dark. Quicker and quicker, the carriage moved along as the screams and moans grew louder. They were soaring along the tracks.

Something soft and sticky touched David's face. He reached his hand up.

"Cobwebs," he said quietly. "The fake kind."

Without warning, the carriage slammed on the brakes and sent him flying forward into the security bar.

They were inside a cave. Red lights glowed all around them. In front of the ride was a large archway with a huge sign.

The music changed tempo. A slow melody, with all the instruments out of tune. David didn't like the music, not at all. He wished his dad was beside him so he could hold his hand again, like when he was seven.

"Get a grip. Nothing bad can happen," David thought. "It's only a fair ride."

He looked around at the stone walls. The sound of water dripping caught his attention. He put out his hand and felt it drop into his palm.

The carriage moved forward again, edging through the archway and into the mouth of hell. The speed picked up as it zoomed around the bend, then began to plummet downwards.

David gripped the skeleton handrail to stop himself from falling forward as they hurtled into the darkness. He nearly jumped out of the carriage when something—a hand?—touched his shoulder.

It happened again, and this time he screamed. The hand, or whatever it was, began squeezing tightly. He released the bar and reached up to his shoulder to see what it was.

There was no hand.

His imagination was in overdrive.

The carriage sped along the tracks, still on a dangerously quick downwards descent. The deeper it went, the darker everything became. The constant bouncing and shaking of the carriage and the relentless wind in his face was getting to him.

The moans and screams all suddenly stopped. So did the blasting, creepy music. He couldn't even hear the boys anymore.

"Ethan?" David said. "Guys, where are you?"

They didn't reply.

The ride came to a stop.

David peered into the darkness. He couldn't make anything out, though he was certain something was out there.

"What now?" David gripped the safety bar tightly with both hands. He waited for the ride to continue, but nothing happened. He was trapped.

Seconds felt like minutes. Minutes like hours.

Then he heard footsteps.

Or slithering?

"Ethan, you there?" he shouted once more.

"Hello, David," a strange voice answered.

David leaned forward in his seat. He didn't recognize the voice.

"Who's there?" he asked.

"Welcome to Hell," the voice answered. "This is your own personal nightmare, David."

A terrible scream cut through the silence. David's hands covered his ears, trying to block it out.

"Not funny, guys," David said, shrinking back in his seat.

The carriage jerked violently and the lights flickered again. David took in his surroundings. From what he could see, sheer rock faces flanked him on either side. Red flowing lava was bubbling just outside the carriage, so close he could feel the immense heat.

A red spotlight blasted him in the face.

David screamed as he realized there were no other carriages. His was the only one.

As his eyes adjusted to the strange red glow, he saw a dark figure moving towards him. He watched it move side to side, up then down, moving inhumanly fast. It was increasing in size as it drew close. It was tall, with its hands outstretched, reaching for him. The lights flashed, and that's when he saw the creature's glowing eyes. And horns.

"I see your friends have all left you alone," the voice whispered in his ear.

David flinched. His eyes darted from left to right,

135

trying to see who—or what?—was speaking to him.

"Who's there?" David shouted. He tried to stand up inside the carriage, but he was stuck.

The spotlight went out.

David started counting, trying to calm his mind while waiting for the lights to come back on. If they did come back on, he dreaded what they would reveal.

He rubbed his sweaty hands on his jeans.

"It's just a ride," David thought. "There's no real danger. You're not seven anymore, dummy. Nothing here can hurt you."

"David," the voice said, now right beside him.

David turned his head.

In the seat next to him was a demon. A monster with red glowing eyes. Horns protruded from the top of his head, and his skin was as black as coal. He had a big evil grin on his face.

"I've been waiting for you, David," the monster said. "Now you're mine."

Piercing cries filled the air.

It took David a moment to realize they were his.

He pulled at the safety bar in front of him,

desperately trying to get off the ride.

"There's no escape, David," the demon said. Placing his hands on David's shoulder, shoving him back into his seat. "Foolish of you to visit, wasn't it? But I knew you wouldn't be able to resist Ethan's taunts."

David shook his head. "This isn't real. It's an illusion. This is a trick. It's all part of the ride." He tried to convince himself this would all be over in a minute, and that he'd see daylight again. Ethan and the boys would be laughing in front of him, and everything would return to normal.

The carriage started to move. Slowly at first, then picking up speed as it blasted through a series of dark tunnels.

The demon sat beside him, laughing and pointing a long scaly finger at him. The hand on his shoulder gripped tighter.

The horrible, out of tune music came back. It pumped through the speakers at an unbearable decibel level. Cries of terror filled his ears. Lights flickered at speed, hurting his eyes.

Without warning, the carriage turned sharply and David saw a gap in the tracks ahead. They were headed towards a ravine. He gripped the bar in front of him and squeezed his eyes shut.

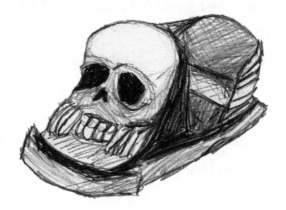

"It's all over," David said. "I'm going to die. I'm going to die."

The carriage slammed to a stop.

David resisted the urge to open his eyes. He could feel the hot breath of the demon on his cheek, and the sharp fingernails were still digging into his shoulder.

Trembling, David slowly peeled back his eyelids. He had to squint as the blinding sunlight hit him directly in the face.

The ride was over.

Breath held, David turned around and looked at the seat beside him.

Empty.

He took a deep breath, raking his hands through his sweaty hair. "I imagined it all," he thought. He was just about to congratulate himself when the voice came back.

"See you soon, David," the same evil voice whispered in his ear.

David panicked and jumped forward, struggling to get out of the carriage.

"The look on your face!" Ethan shouted as he pointed at David. "Did you see a ghost?"

"He looks terrified," said Mathew, one of the other boys.

"No, I'm not," David said, still breathing hard. There was a loud *click* sound, the release button, and he was finally able to move the security bar that held the passengers to their seat.

The awful voice was still inside his head.

"See you soon, David," it whispered. "I've marked you. You're mine."

David looked all around, but there was nothing there. His stomach was in knots. All those horrible screams still echoed in his ears as he climbed from the ride and joined his friends.

"Cool ride, wasn't it?" Matthew said. "All those cobwebs were annoying, but that banshee lady screaming like that?" He rubbed his ears. "She screams louder than my little sister."

David listened as the boys recounted their experience on the Ghost Train of Horror. It was completely different from his hellish experience.

David turned back to look at the ride one last time.

Standing beside the carriage was the man dressed as a zombie. He smiled at David. Then his face changed. His human face twisted into the face of a monster.

Pointing to himself, he gestured that David now belonged to him. Then he tapped his wrist and mouthed one word to him.

"Midnight."

"Let's get outta here," David said as he walked away, fast as he could.

"Wait up!" Matthew said.

"What's all over your pants?" Ethan asked, pointing. "And your hands, too."

David looked at his hands. They were stained red. His trousers were covered in it too. He thought back to the dripping water in the cave.

"Looks like blood," Matthew said. "How come we didn't get any?"

David didn't hear a word. The shock of who he had just met had him in a nearly catatonic state as they all walked home.

The devil had marked him as one of his own.

All the way back to his house, David hardly said a word. He didn't even wave goodbye when they all headed home in different directions. He needed to get home, where he'd be safe.

You're mine

Midnight

It was already 5:53pm. Only six hours, six minutes, six seconds…until midnight.

THE END

ABOUT THE AUTHOR

Amanda J Evans writes paranormal and fantasy novels as well as children's stories. Amanda lives in Oldcastle, Co. Meath, Ireland with her husband and two children. She is known locally by her married name Donnelly, and her daughter Emma is the illustrator for this book. Amanda has been writing since a very young age, when she would create stories to share with her friends, and at times terrify them. She was published in several journals and anthologies in 2016 and 2017. Her first novel *Finding Forever* was self-published in 2017 and her second novel *Save Her Soul* released on August 1st 2017. Amanda is currently working on several books, including a middle grade novel for 2018. You can find out more on her website www.amandajevans.com and her social media sites

MEET THE ILLUSTRATOR

Emma Donnelly is a fourteen-year-old artist and animator from Ireland. This was her first illustration project with her mom. Emma's goal is to become a famous animator, creating her own anime productions. Emma has been drawing for several years and has moved into editing and animation also. She has a following on Instagram and is currently working hard on mastering her skills.

THANK YOU

Thank you for purchasing and reading *Nightmare Realities: Scary Stories for Dark Nights.*

Handersen Publishing is an independent publishing house that specializes in creating quality young adult, middle grade, and picture books.

We hope you enjoyed this book and will consider leaving a review on Goodreads or Amazon. A small review can make a big difference for the little guys.

Thank you.

Prior publication

"All Hallows Eve." *Stinkwaves—a magazine for young readers.* Vol. 4 (2) 2016.

MORE GREAT BOOKS FROM
HANDERSEN PUBLISHING

Also from Handersen Publishing

Cover Art By
Sandeep Kumar Mishra

Fantastical Gravestones
Herb Kauderer

Featured Artists
Emma Donnelly
Dusty Grein
Jane Gregoritch
Raven Howell
Denny E Marshall
Sandeep Kumar Mishra
Tempus Serene
Cesar Valtierra

Featured Poets
Amanda J Evans
Raven Howell
Herb Kauderer
Denny E Marshall
Peter MacQuarrie
Philippa Rae
Jordan Tucker
Sephonē Zorro

Featured Authors
Malena Bertrand
Dusty Grein
Herb Kauderer
Jonathan Kemmerer-Scovner
Rebecca Linam
Liam Martin
Alessia Mattei
Sophie O'Brien
Sofia Schlozman
Jason Stussy
Jeffrey Wald
Jacqueline West
Sayuri Yamada

Stinkwaves
Magazine
Fall 2017
Volume 5 Issue 2

Stinkwaves started in 2013 as a zine, but has now grown into a "mega-zine" filled with the works of talented indie authors, poets & illustrators. Each issue is packed with short stories, flash fiction, poetry, illustrations, and author interviews.

www.stinkwavesmagazine.com

Handersen Publishing

Great books for young readers

www.handersenpublishing.com

CPSIA information can be obtained
at www.ICGtesting.com
Printed in the USA
BVHW04*1936190418
513224BV00017B/62/P